# PLANTS VS. ZOMBIES™

## BULLY FOR YOU #1



[redacted]

ABDO Spotlight
DARK HORSE COMICS
PopCap

Written by **PAUL TOBIN**
Art by **RON CHAN**
Colors by **MATTHEW J. RAINWATER**
Letters by **STEVE DUTRO**
Cover by **RON CHAN**

President and Publisher **MIKE RICHARDSON**
Editor **PHILIP R. SIMON**
Assistant Editor **ROXY POLK**
Designer **KAT LARSON**
Digital Production **CHRISTINA McKENZIE**

Special thanks to LEIGH BEACH, GARY CLAY, SHANA DOERR, A.J. RATHBUN, KRISTEN STAR, JEREMY VANHOOZER, and everyone at PopCap Games.

DarkHorse.com | PopCap.com

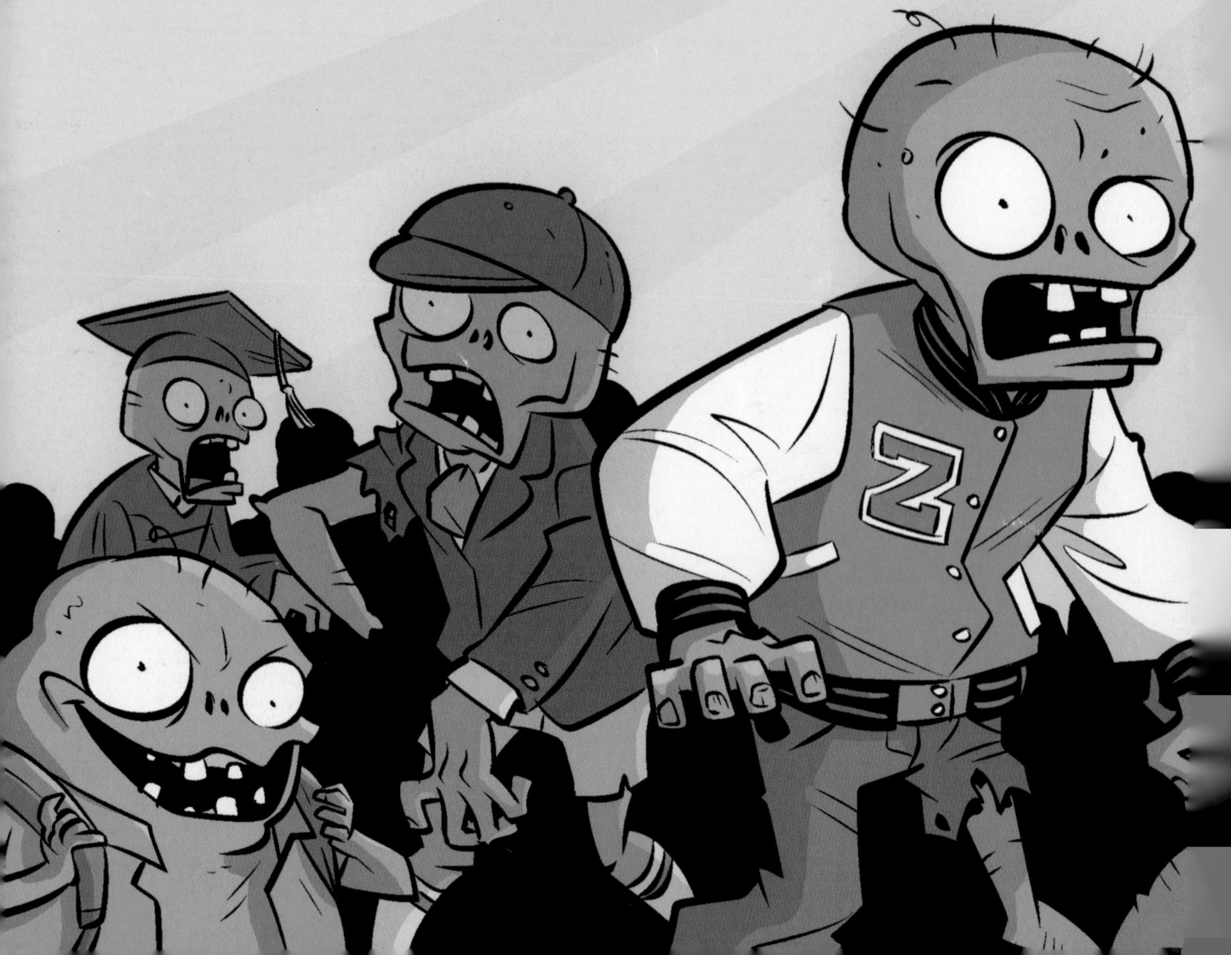
Z

# PLANTS VS. ZOMBIES™

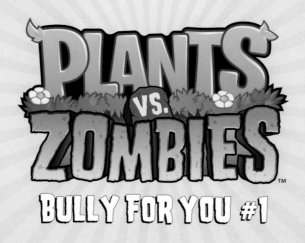

## BULLY FOR YOU #1

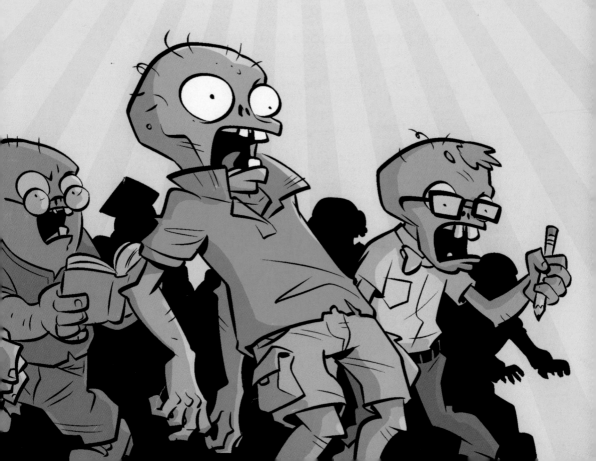

**ABDOPUBLISHING.COM**

Reinforced library bound edition published in 2017 by Spotlight, a division of ABDO, PO Box 398166, Minneapolis, Minnesota 55439. Spotlight produces high-quality reinforced library bound editions for schools and libraries.
Published by agreement with Dark Horse Comics.

Printed in the United States of America, North Mankato, Minnesota.
042016
092016

THIS BOOK CONTAINS RECYCLED MATERIALS

Originally issued as Plants vs. Zombies: Bully for You #1 by Dark Horse Comics in 2015.

**PUBLISHER'S CATALOGING IN PUBLICATION DATA**

Names: Tobin, Paul, author. | Chan, Ron ; Rainwater, Matthew J., illustrators.
Title: Bully for you / by Paul Tobin ; illustrated by Ron Chan and Matthew J. Rainwater.
Description: Minneapolis, MN : Spotlight, [2017] | Series: Plants vs. zombies
Summary: Caught in the middle of zombie warfare, Nate and Patrice must join forces with Crazy Dave to beat them but could Crazy Dave's ice cream obsession save the day?
Identifiers: LCCN 2016934735 | ISBN 9781614795346 (v.1 : lib. bdg.) | ISBN 9781614795353 (v.2 : lib. bdg.) | ISBN 9781614795360 (v.3 : lib. bdg.)
Subjects: LCSH: Bullying--Juvenile fiction. | Plants--Juvenile fiction. | Zombies--Juvenile fiction. | Adventure and adventurers--Juvenile fiction. | Comic books strips, etc.--Juvenile fiction. | Graphic novels--Juvenile fiction.
Classification: DDC 741.5--dc23
LC record available at http://lccn.loc.gov/2016934735

Spotlight

A Division of ABDO
abdopublishing.com

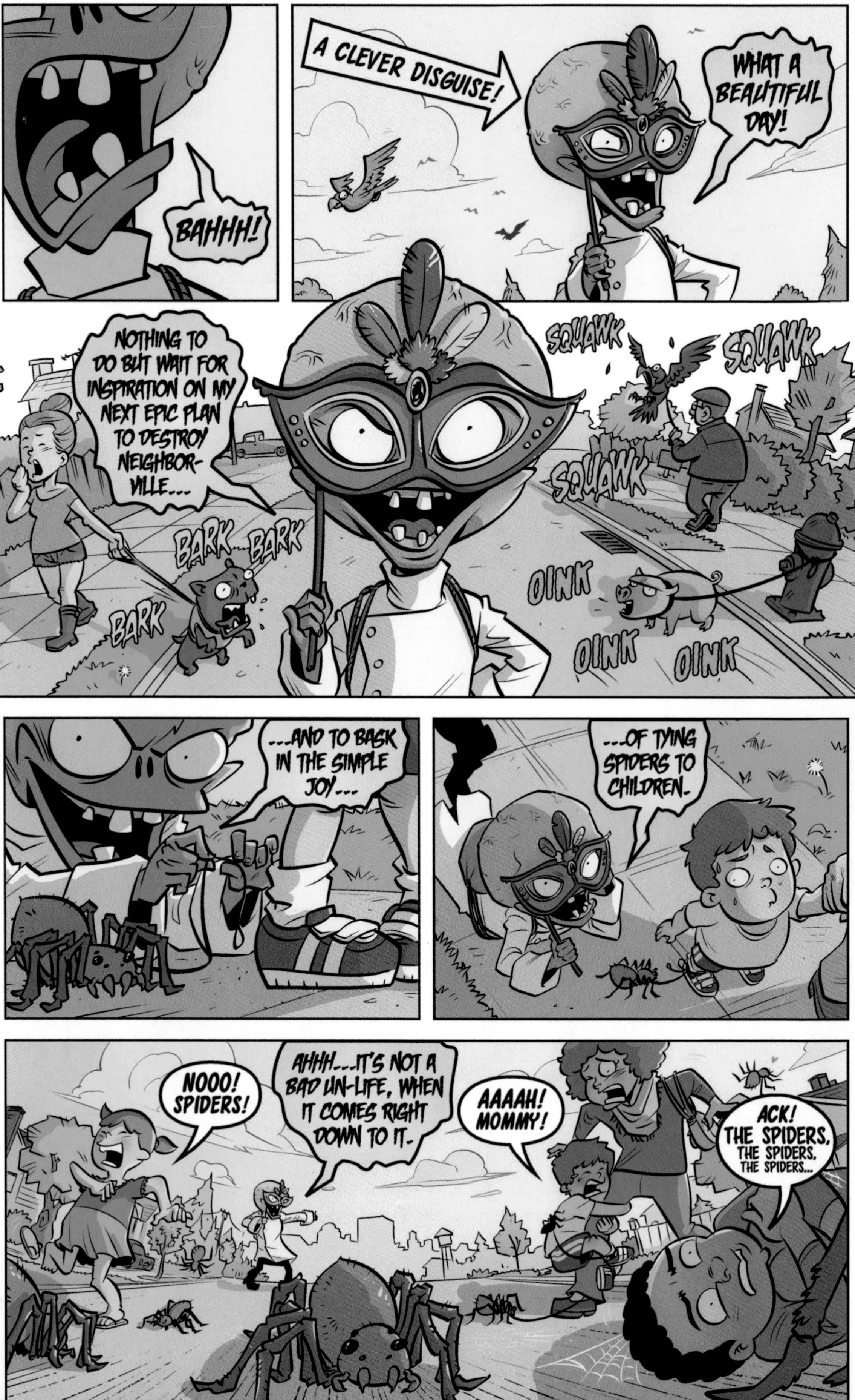
BAHHH!
A CLEVER DISGUISE!
WHAT A BEAUTIFUL DAY!
NOTHING TO DO BUT WAIT FOR INSPIRATION ON MY NEXT EPIC PLAN TO DESTROY NEIGHBOR-VILLE...
SQUAWK
SQUAWK
SQUAWK
BARK
BARK
BARK
OINK
OINK
OINK
...AND TO BASK IN THE SIMPLE JOY...
...OF TYING SPIDERS TO CHILDREN.
NOOO! SPIDERS!
AHHH...IT'S NOT A BAD UN-LIFE, WHEN IT COMES RIGHT DOWN TO IT.
AAAAH! MOMMY!
ACK! THE SPIDERS, THE SPIDERS, THE SPIDERS...

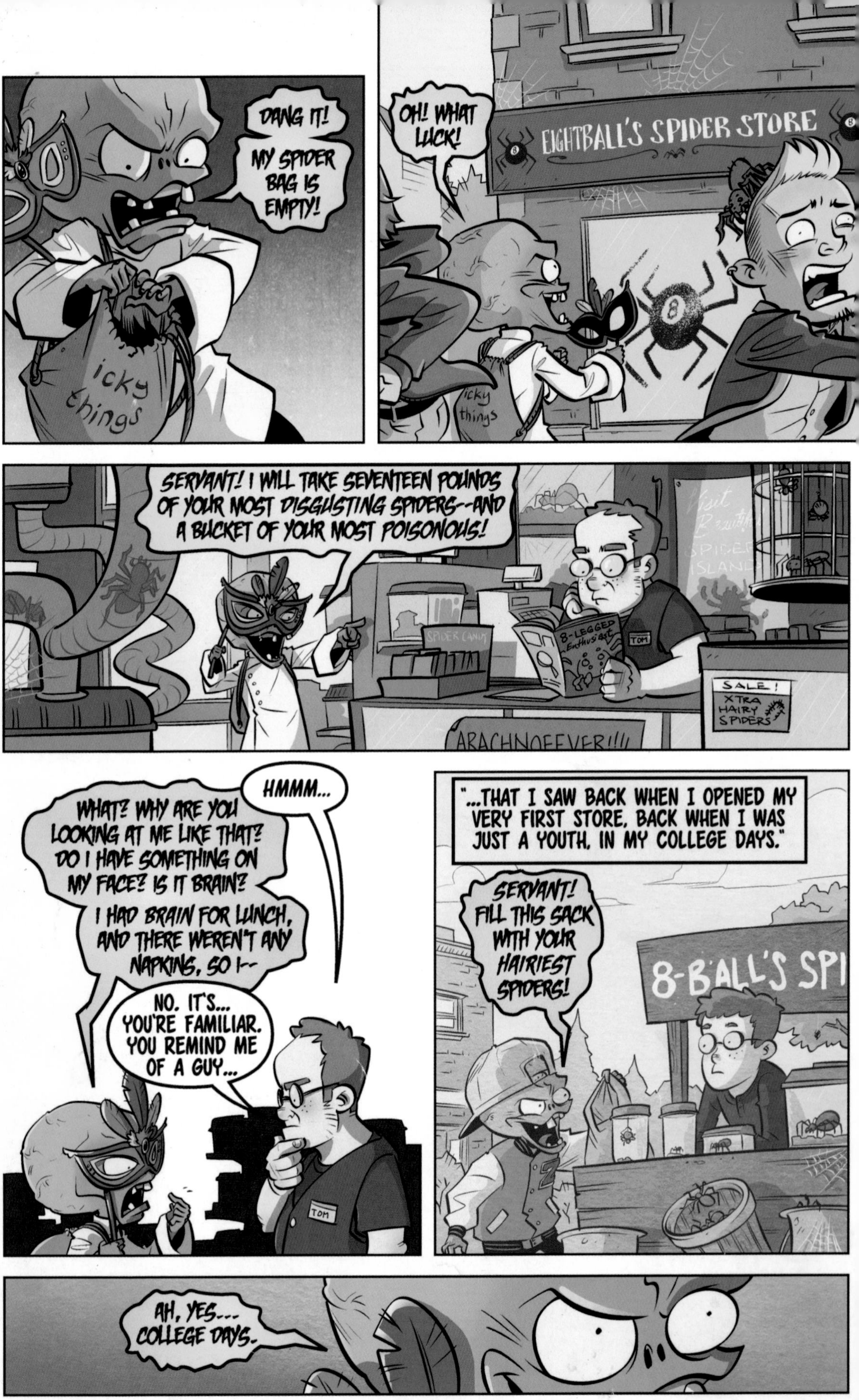
DANG IT!
MY SPIDER BAG IS EMPTY!
icky things
OH! WHAT LUCK!
EIGHTBALL'S SPIDER STORE
SERVANT! I WILL TAKE SEVENTEEN POUNDS OF YOUR MOST DISGUSTING SPIDERS--AND A BUCKET OF YOUR MOST POISONOUS!
SPIDER CANDY
8-LEGGED Enthusiast
TOM
SALE! XTRA HAIRY SPIDERS
ARACHNOFEVER!!!
HMMM...
WHAT? WHY ARE YOU LOOKING AT ME LIKE THAT? DO I HAVE SOMETHING ON MY FACE? IS IT BRAIN?
I HAD BRAIN FOR LUNCH, AND THERE WEREN'T ANY NAPKINS, SO I--
NO. IT'S... YOU'RE FAMILIAR. YOU REMIND ME OF A GUY...
TOM
"...THAT I SAW BACK WHEN I OPENED MY VERY FIRST STORE, BACK WHEN I WAS JUST A YOUTH, IN MY COLLEGE DAYS."
SERVANT! FILL THIS SACK WITH YOUR HAIRIEST SPIDERS!
8-BALL'S SPI
AH, YES... COLLEGE DAYS.

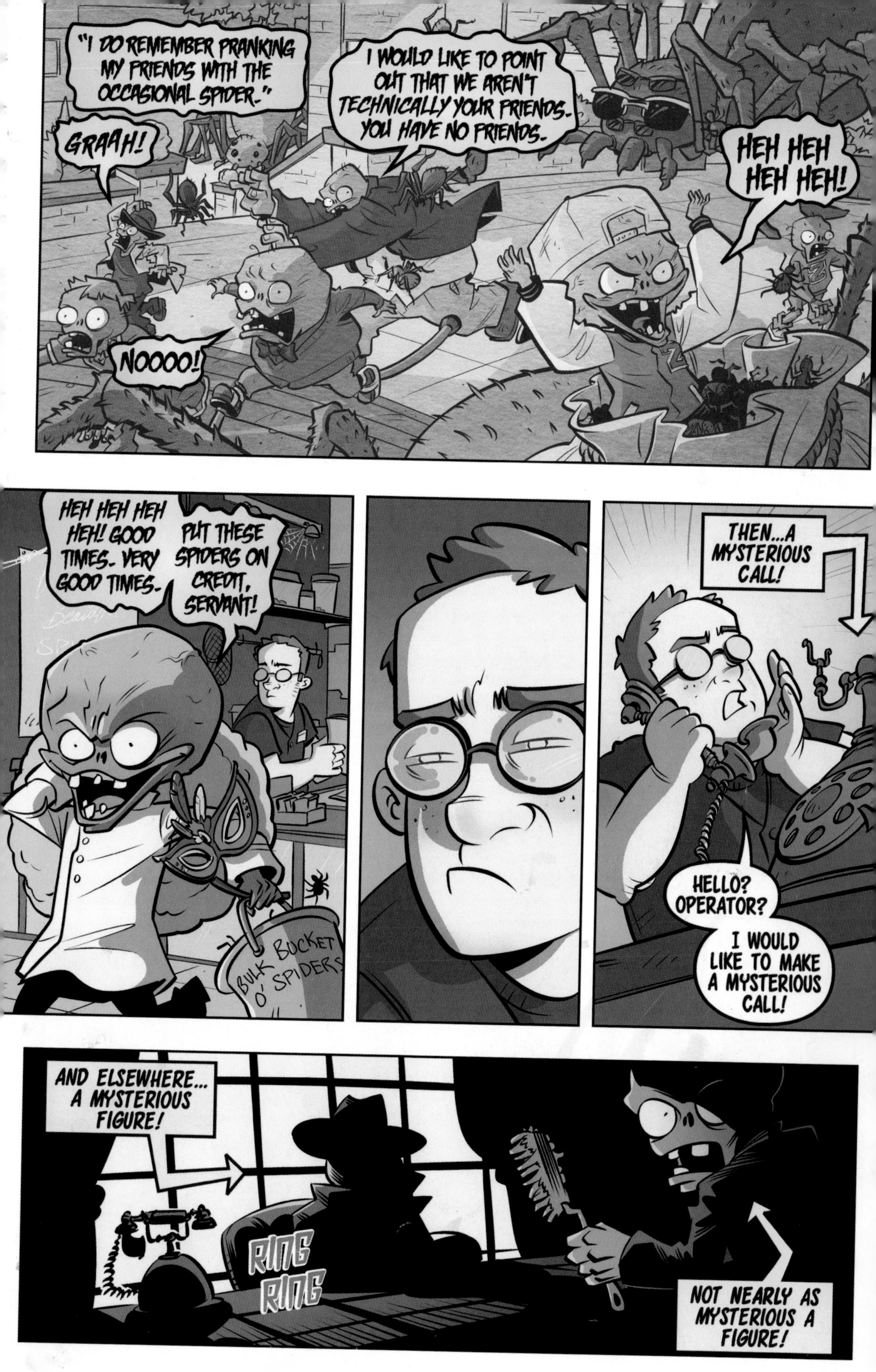
"I DO REMEMBER PRANKING MY FRIENDS WITH THE OCCASIONAL SPIDER."
GRAAH!
I WOULD LIKE TO POINT OUT THAT WE AREN'T TECHNICALLY YOUR FRIENDS. YOU HAVE NO FRIENDS.
HEH HEH HEH HEH!
NOOOO!
HEH HEH HEH HEH! GOOD TIMES. VERY GOOD TIMES.
PUT THESE SPIDERS ON CREDIT, SERVANT!
BULK BUCKET O' SPIDERS
THEN...A MYSTERIOUS CALL!
HELLO? OPERATOR?
I WOULD LIKE TO MAKE A MYSTERIOUS CALL!
AND ELSEWHERE... A MYSTERIOUS FIGURE!
RING RING
NOT NEARLY AS MYSTERIOUS A FIGURE!

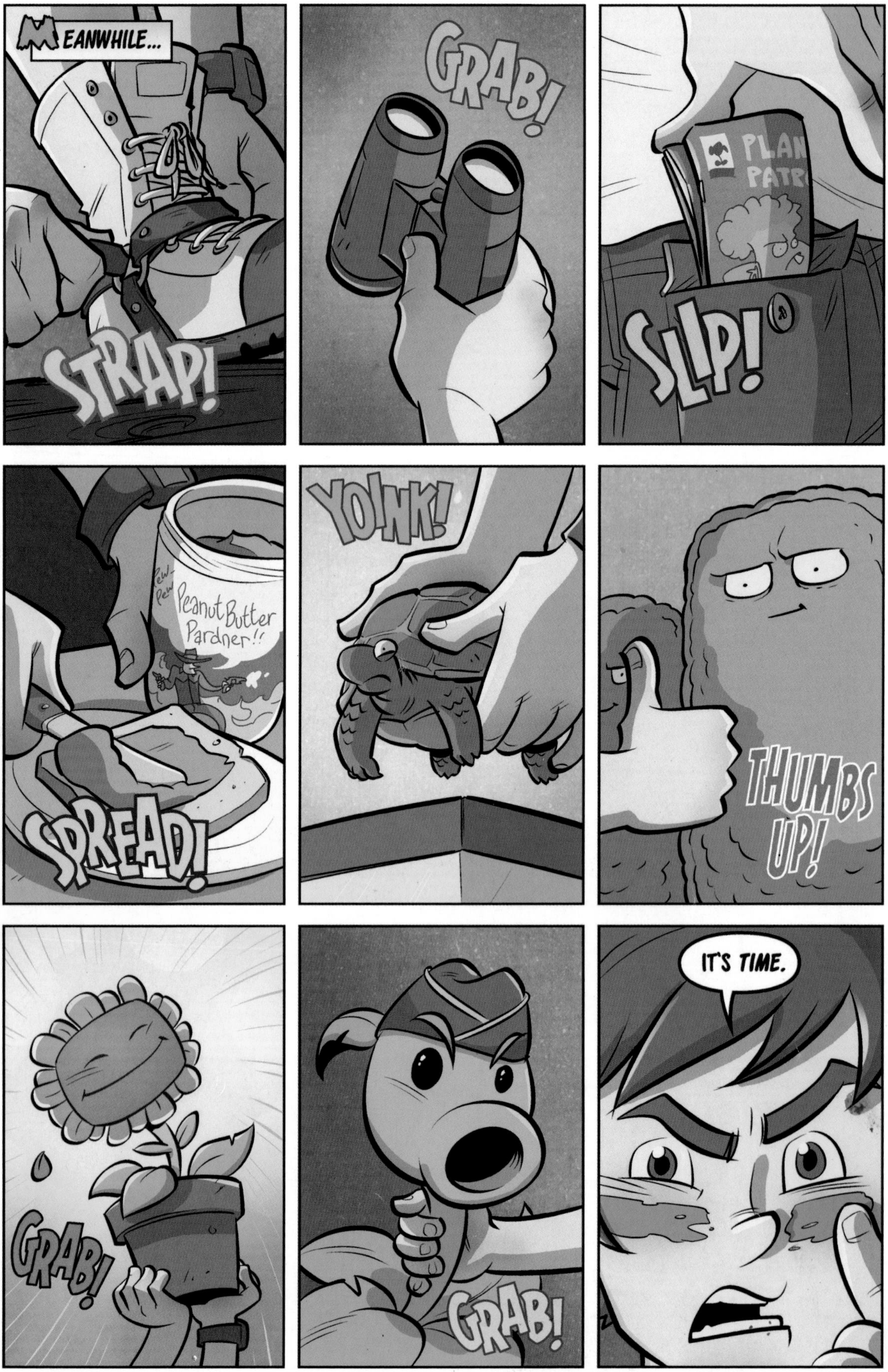
MEANWHILE...
STRAP!
GRAB!
SLIP!
Pew-Pew
Peanut Butter Pardner!!
SPREAD!
YOINK!
THUMBS UP!
GRAB!
GRAB!
IT'S TIME.

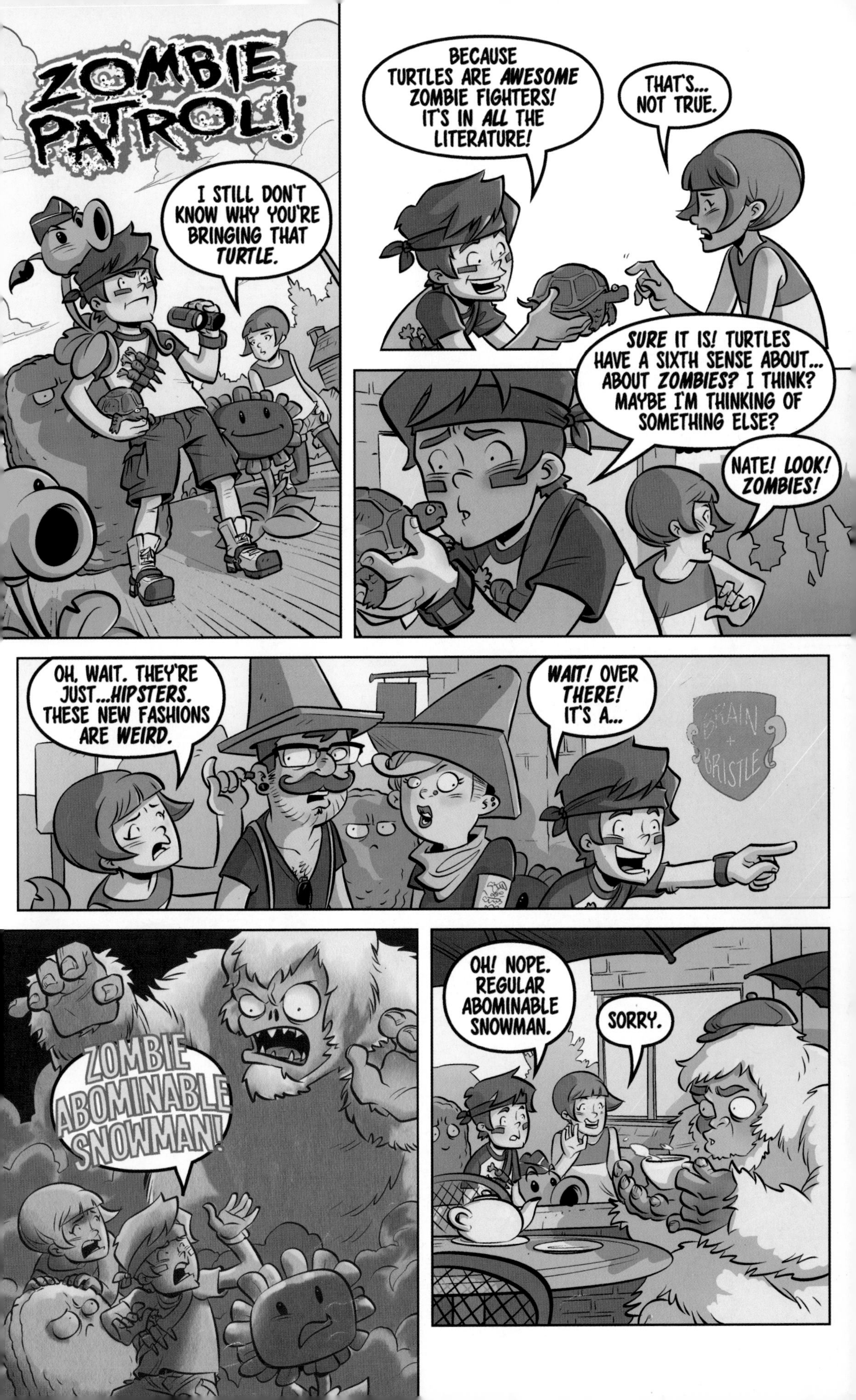
ZOMBIE PATROL!
I STILL DON'T KNOW WHY YOU'RE BRINGING THAT *TURTLE.*
BECAUSE TURTLES ARE *AWESOME* ZOMBIE FIGHTERS! IT'S IN *ALL* THE LITERATURE!
THAT'S... NOT TRUE.
*SURE* IT IS! TURTLES HAVE A SIXTH SENSE ABOUT... ABOUT *ZOMBIES?* I THINK? MAYBE I'M THINKING OF SOMETHING ELSE?
NATE! *LOOK! ZOMBIES!*
OH, WAIT. THEY'RE JUST...*HIPSTERS.* THESE NEW FASHIONS ARE *WEIRD.*
*WAIT!* OVER *THERE!* IT'S A...
BRAIN + BRISTLE
ZOMBIE ABOMINABLE SNOWMAN!
OH! NOPE. REGULAR ABOMINABLE SNOWMAN.
SORRY.

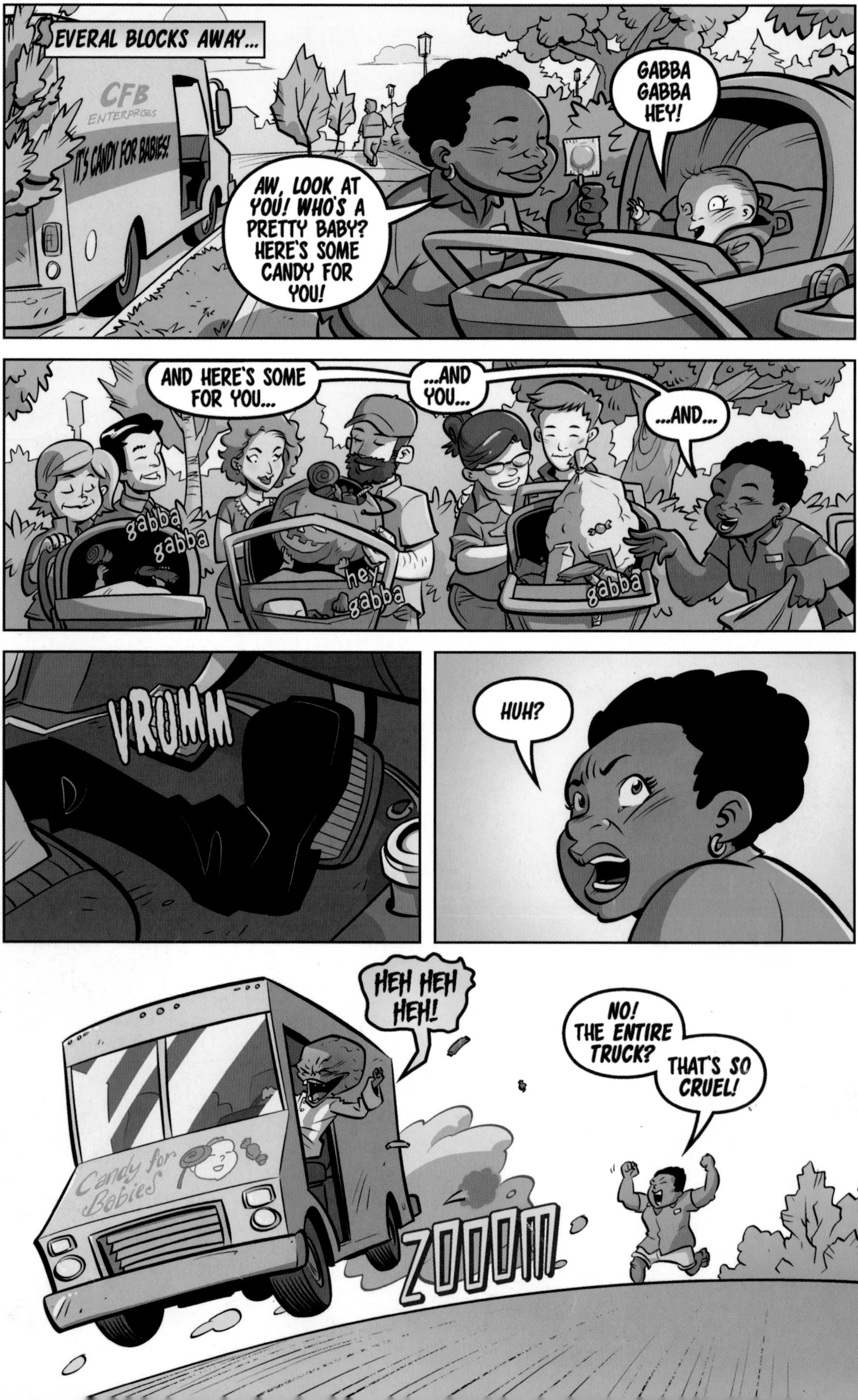
SEVERAL BLOCKS AWAY...
CFB ENTERPRISES
IT'S CANDY FOR BABIES!
GABBA GABBA HEY!
AW, LOOK AT YOU! WHO'S A PRETTY BABY? HERE'S SOME CANDY FOR YOU!
AND HERE'S SOME FOR YOU...
...AND YOU...
...AND...
gabba gabba
hey gabba
gabba
VROMM
HUH?
HEH HEH HEH!
NO! THE ENTIRE TRUCK?
THAT'S SO CRUEL!
Candy for Babies
ZOOOM

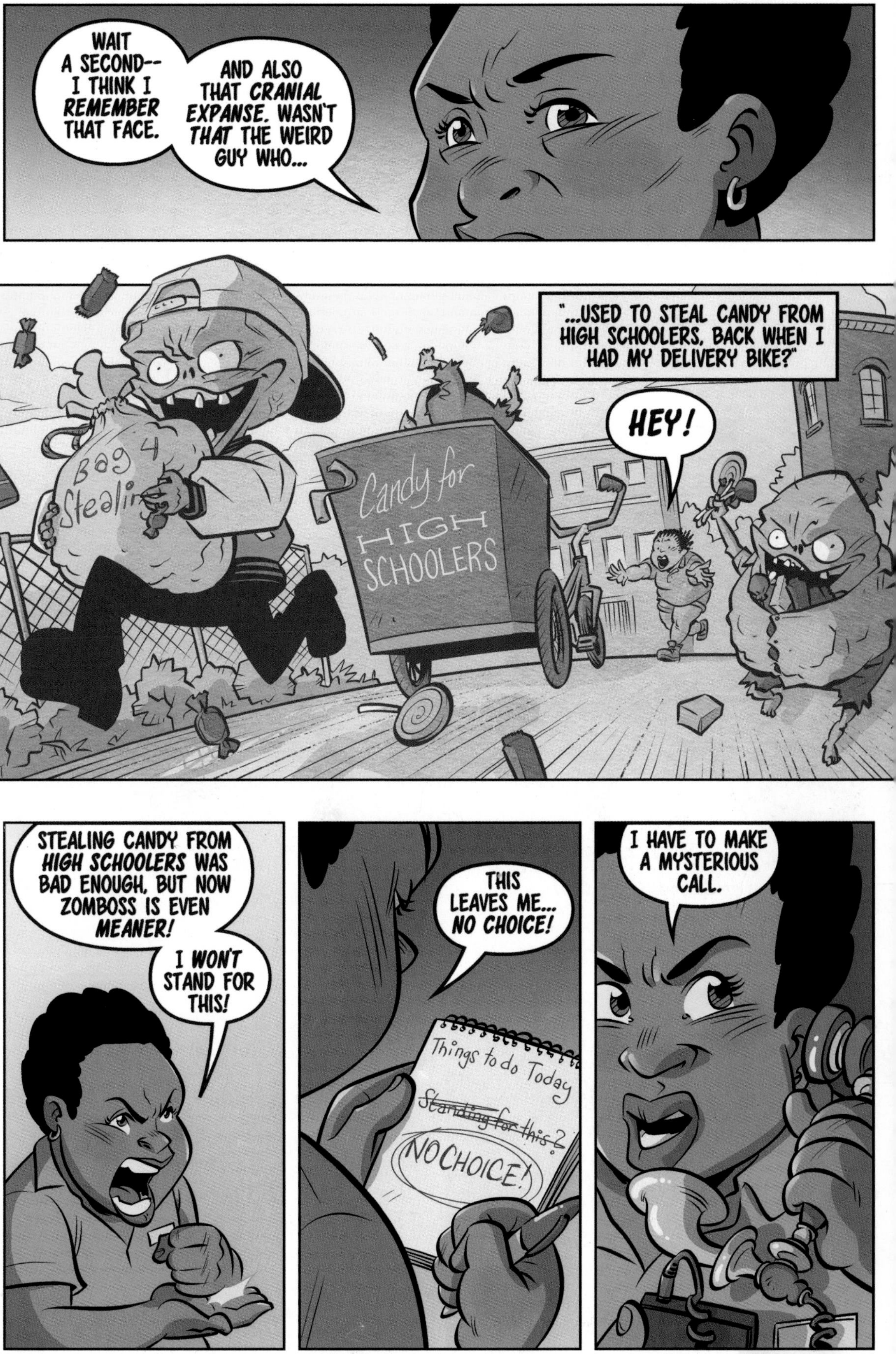
WAIT A SECOND-- I THINK I REMEMBER THAT FACE.
AND ALSO THAT CRANIAL EXPANSE. WASN'T THAT THE WEIRD GUY WHO...
"...USED TO STEAL CANDY FROM HIGH SCHOOLERS, BACK WHEN I HAD MY DELIVERY BIKE?"
HEY!
Bag 4 Stealin
Candy for HIGH SCHOOLERS
STEALING CANDY FROM HIGH SCHOOLERS WAS BAD ENOUGH, BUT NOW ZOMBOSS IS EVEN MEANER!
I WON'T STAND FOR THIS!
THIS LEAVES ME... NO CHOICE!
Things to do Today
~~Standing for this?~~
NO CHOICE!
I HAVE TO MAKE A MYSTERIOUS CALL.

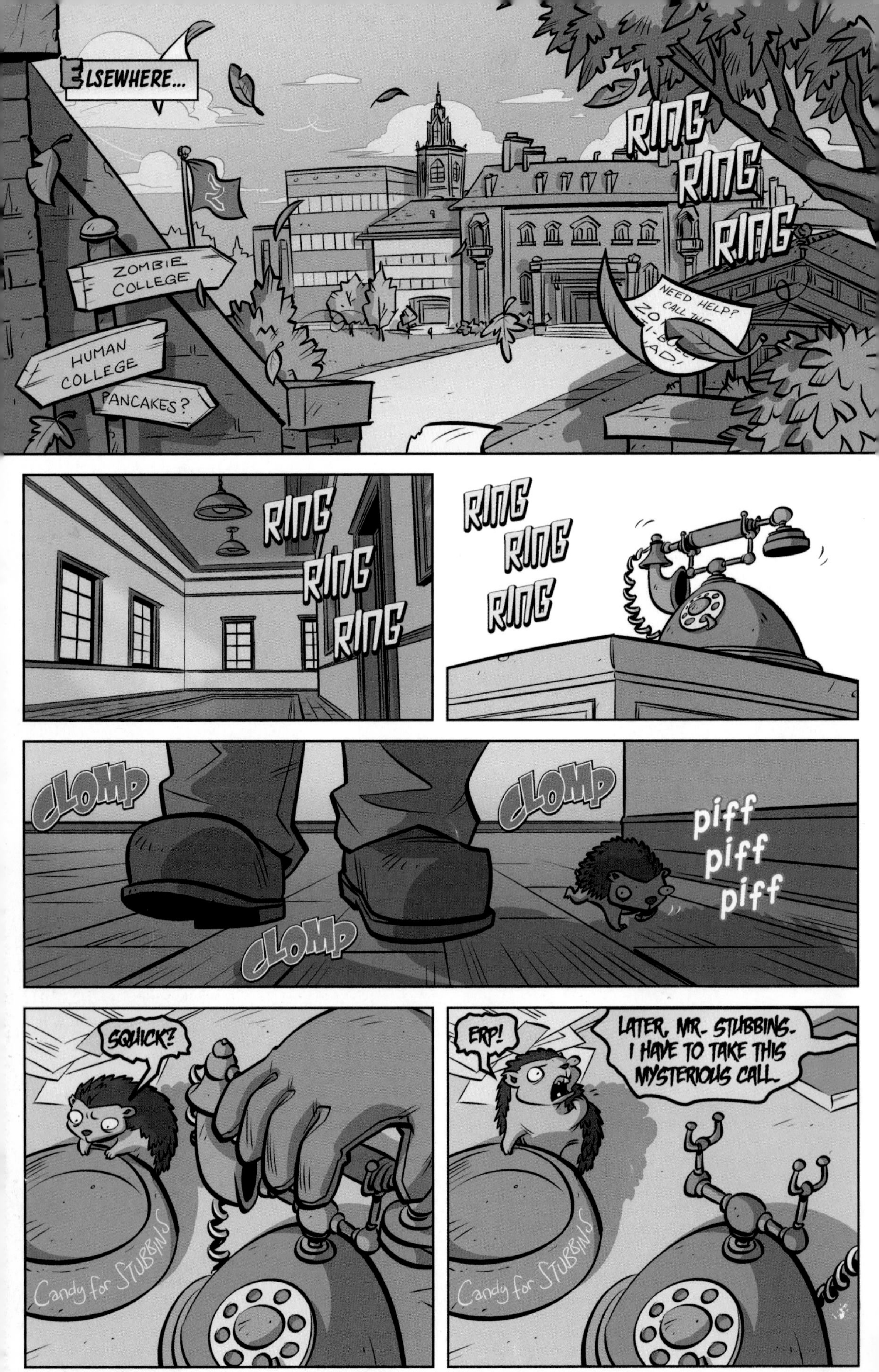
ELSEWHERE...
ZOMBIE COLLEGE
HUMAN COLLEGE
PANCAKES?
NEED HELP? CALL THE
RING RING RING
RING RING RING
RING RING RING
CLOMP
CLOMP
CLOMP
piff piff piff
SQUICK?
Candy for STUBBINS
ERP!
LATER, MR. STUBBINS. I HAVE TO TAKE THIS MYSTERIOUS CALL.
Candy for STUBBINS

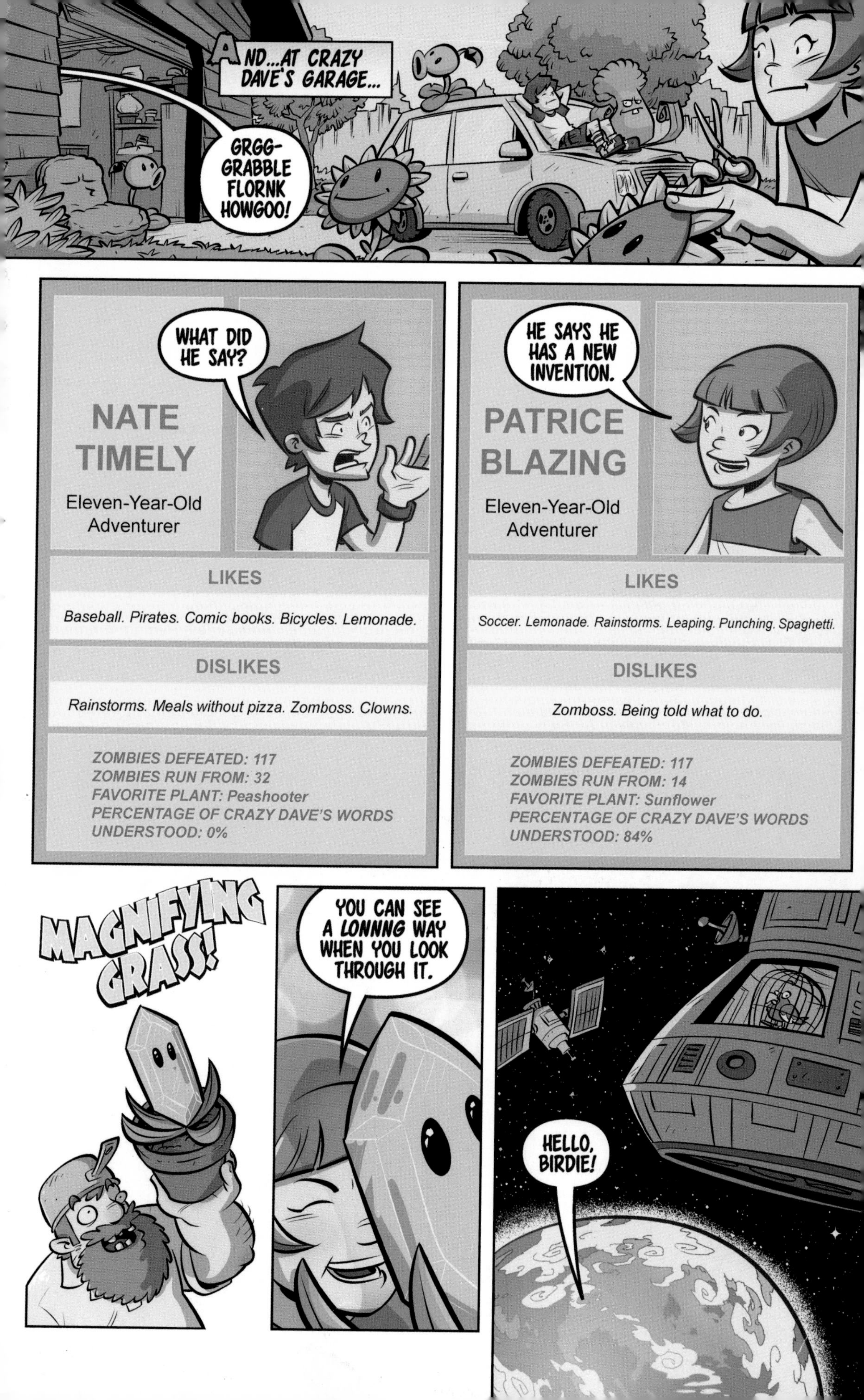
AND...AT CRAZY DAVE'S GARAGE...
GRGG-GRABBLE FLORNK HOWGOO!
WHAT DID HE SAY?
NATE TIMELY
Eleven-Year-Old Adventurer
LIKES
Baseball. Pirates. Comic books. Bicycles. Lemonade.
DISLIKES
Rainstorms. Meals without pizza. Zomboss. Clowns.
ZOMBIES DEFEATED: 117
ZOMBIES RUN FROM: 32
FAVORITE PLANT: Peashooter
PERCENTAGE OF CRAZY DAVE'S WORDS UNDERSTOOD: 0%
HE SAYS HE HAS A NEW INVENTION.
PATRICE BLAZING
Eleven-Year-Old Adventurer
LIKES
Soccer. Lemonade. Rainstorms. Leaping. Punching. Spaghetti.
DISLIKES
Zomboss. Being told what to do.
ZOMBIES DEFEATED: 117
ZOMBIES RUN FROM: 14
FAVORITE PLANT: Sunflower
PERCENTAGE OF CRAZY DAVE'S WORDS UNDERSTOOD: 84%
MAGNIFYING GRASS!
YOU CAN SEE A LONNNG WAY WHEN YOU LOOK THROUGH IT.
HELLO, BIRDIE!

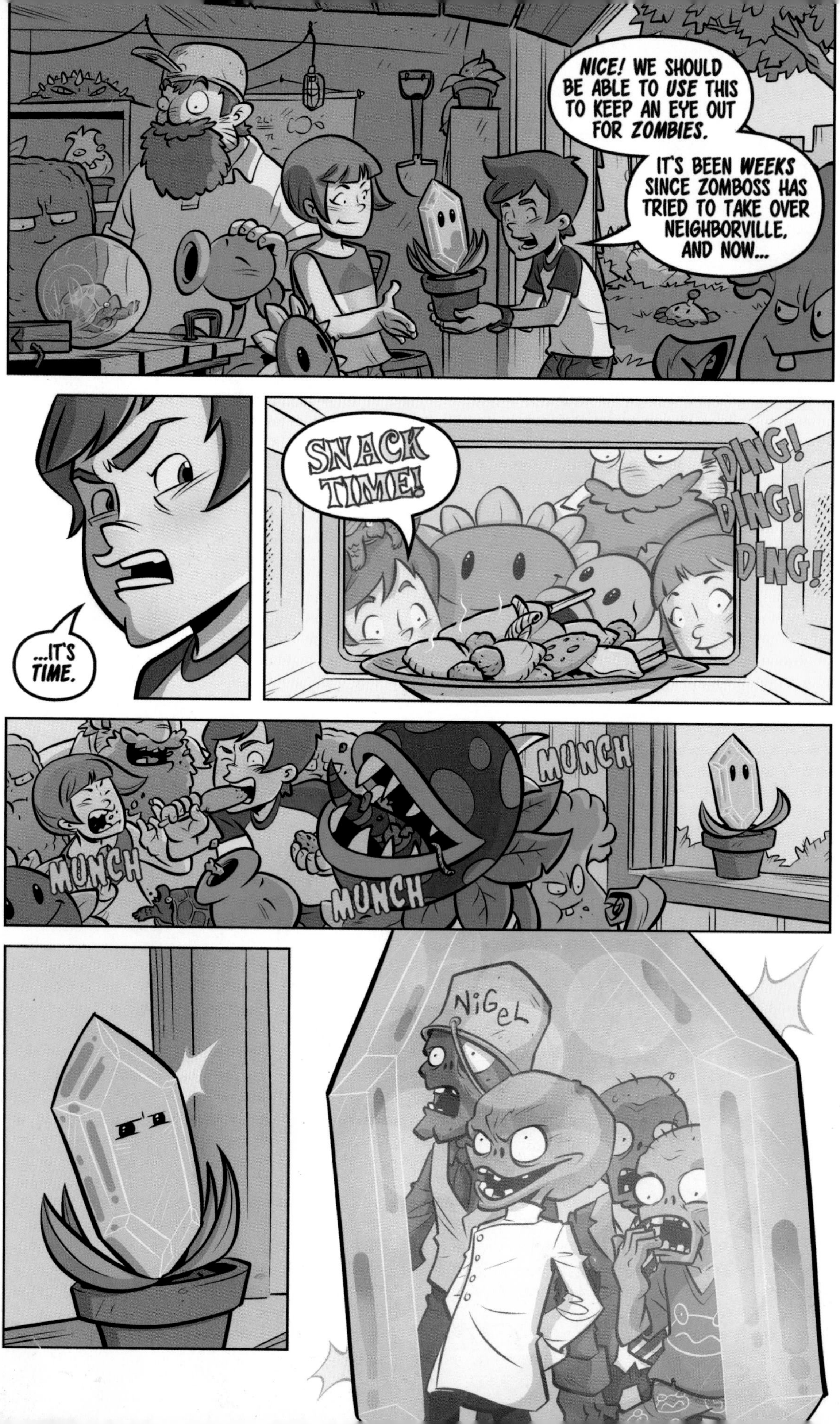
NICE! WE SHOULD BE ABLE TO USE THIS TO KEEP AN EYE OUT FOR ZOMBIES.
IT'S BEEN WEEKS SINCE ZOMBOSS HAS TRIED TO TAKE OVER NEIGHBORVILLE, AND NOW...
...IT'S TIME.
SNACK TIME!
DING! DING! DING!
MUNCH
MUNCH
MUNCH
NiGeL

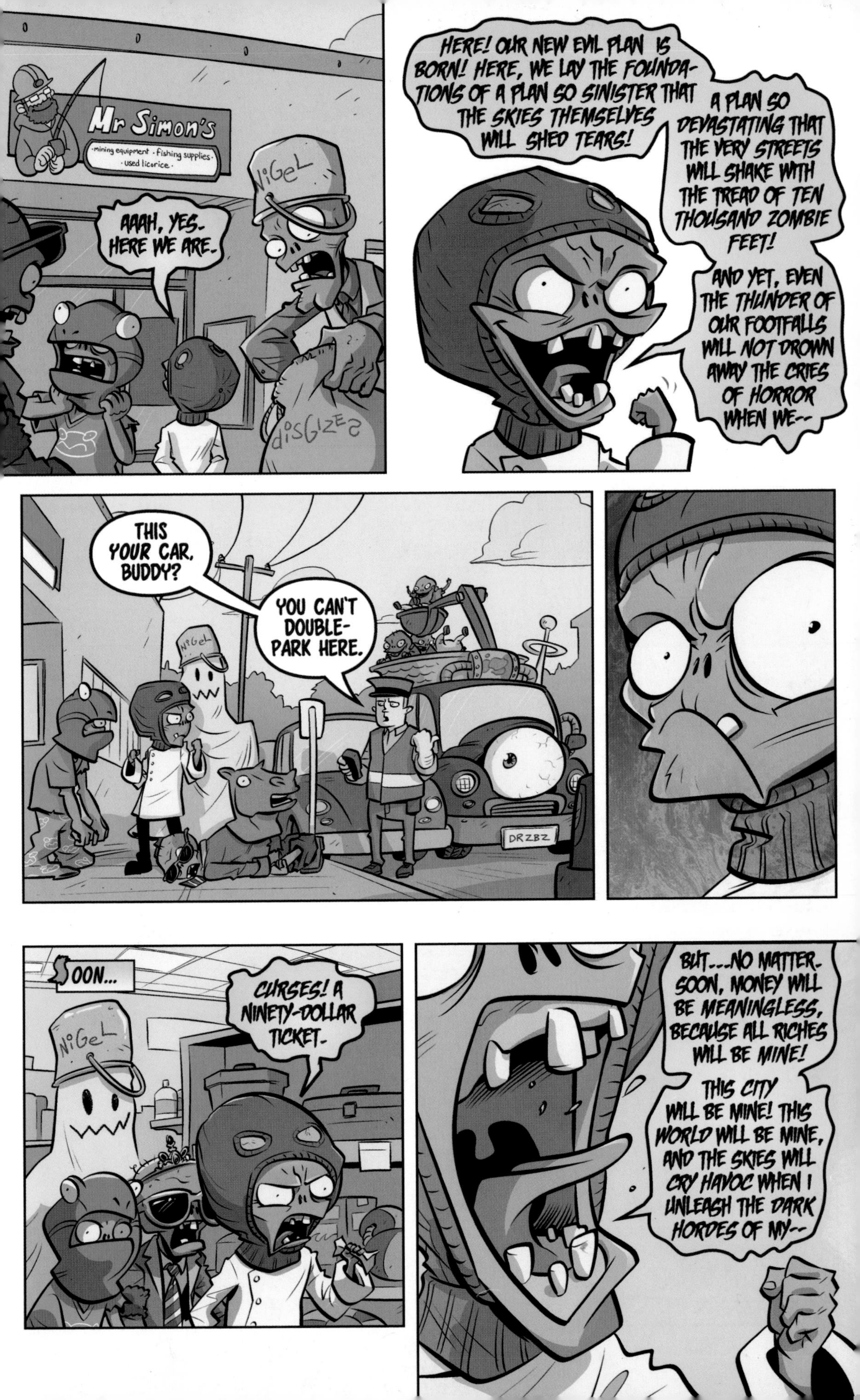
Mr Simon's
·mining equipment · fishing supplies · ·used licorice·
NiGeL
AAAH, YES. HERE WE ARE.
disGIZES
HERE! OUR NEW EVIL PLAN IS BORN! HERE, WE LAY THE FOUNDATIONS OF A PLAN SO SINISTER THAT THE SKIES THEMSELVES WILL SHED TEARS!
A PLAN SO DEVASTATING THAT THE VERY STREETS WILL SHAKE WITH THE TREAD OF TEN THOUSAND ZOMBIE FEET!
AND YET, EVEN THE THUNDER OF OUR FOOTFALLS WILL NOT DROWN AWAY THE CRIES OF HORROR WHEN WE--
THIS YOUR CAR, BUDDY?
YOU CAN'T DOUBLE-PARK HERE.
NiGeL
DRZBZ
SOON...
NiGeL
CURSES! A NINETY-DOLLAR TICKET.
BUT...NO MATTER. SOON, MONEY WILL BE MEANINGLESS, BECAUSE ALL RICHES WILL BE MINE!
THIS CITY WILL BE MINE! THIS WORLD WILL BE MINE, AND THE SKIES WILL CRY HAVOC WHEN I UNLEASH THE DARK HORDES OF MY--

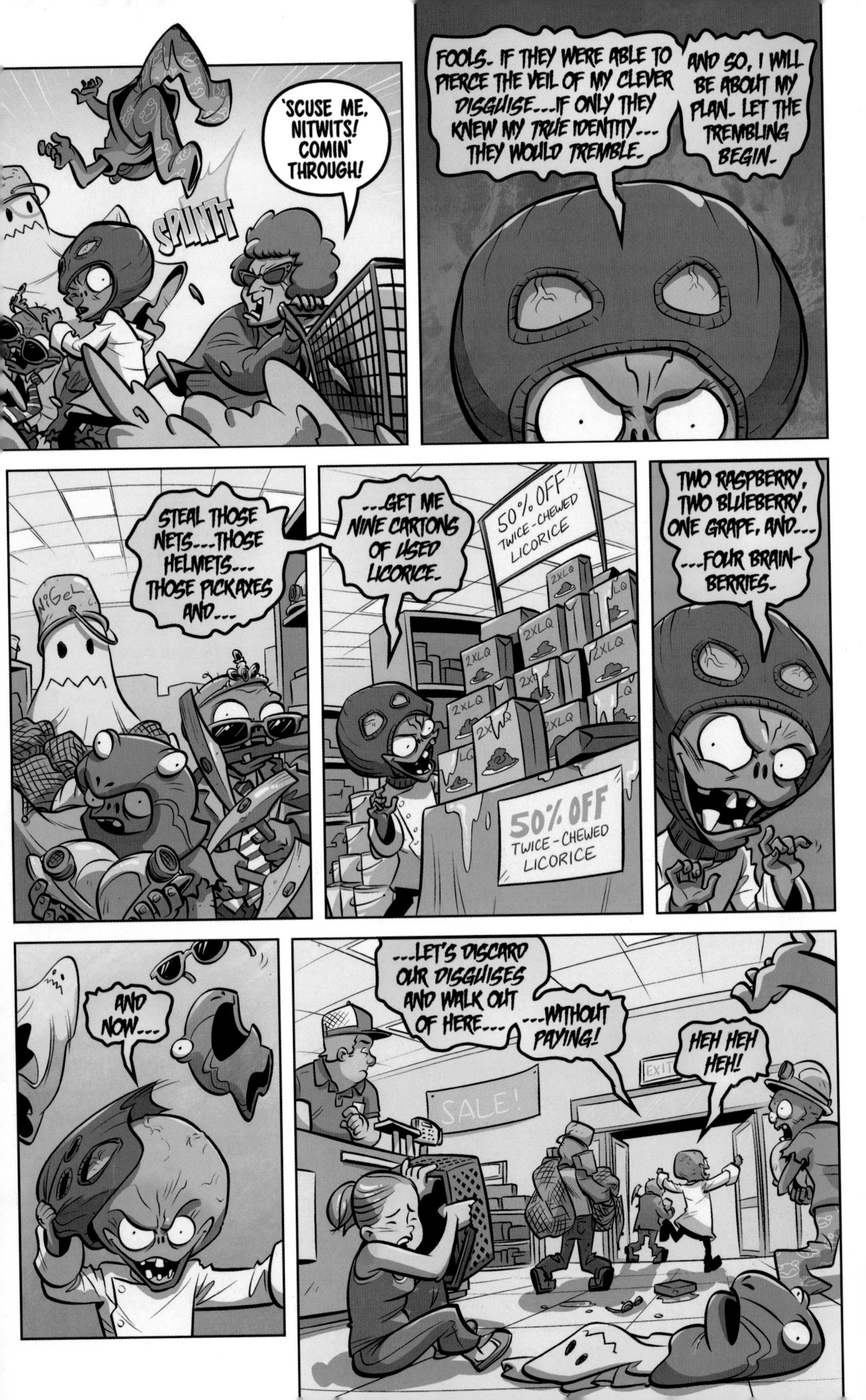

SPLNTT
'SCUSE ME, NITWITS! COMIN' THROUGH!
FOOLS. IF THEY WERE ABLE TO PIERCE THE VEIL OF MY CLEVER DISGUISE...IF ONLY THEY KNEW MY TRUE IDENTITY... THEY WOULD TREMBLE.
AND SO, I WILL BE ABOUT MY PLAN. LET THE TREMBLING BEGIN.
STEAL THOSE NETS...THOSE HELMETS... THOSE PICKAXES AND...
NIGEL
...GET ME NINE CARTONS OF USED LICORICE.
50% OFF TWICE-CHEWED LICORICE
2XLQ
50% OFF TWICE-CHEWED LICORICE
TWO RASPBERRY, TWO BLUEBERRY, ONE GRAPE, AND...
...FOUR BRAIN-BERRIES.
AND NOW...
...LET'S DISCARD OUR DISGUISES AND WALK OUT OF HERE...
...WITHOUT PAYING!
SALE!
EXIT
HEH HEH HEH!

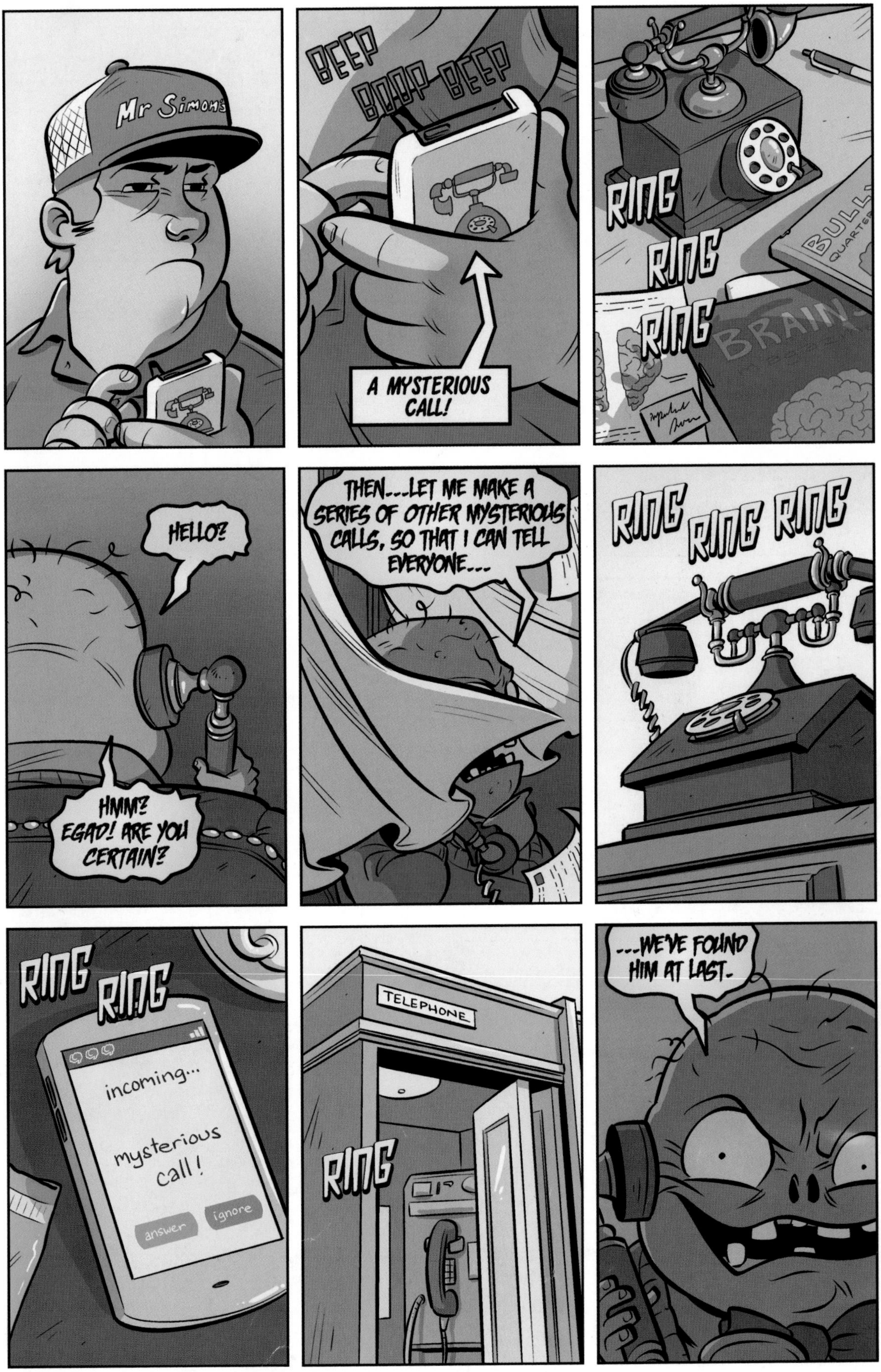
Mr Simon's
BEEP
BOOP BEEP
A MYSTERIOUS CALL!
RING
RING
RING
BULL
QUARTER
BRAINS
HELLO?
HMM? EGAD! ARE YOU CERTAIN?
THEN...LET ME MAKE A SERIES OF OTHER MYSTERIOUS CALLS, SO THAT I CAN TELL EVERYONE...
RING
RING RING
RING
RING
incoming...
mysterious call!
answer
ignore
TELEPHONE
RING
...WE'VE FOUND HIM AT LAST.

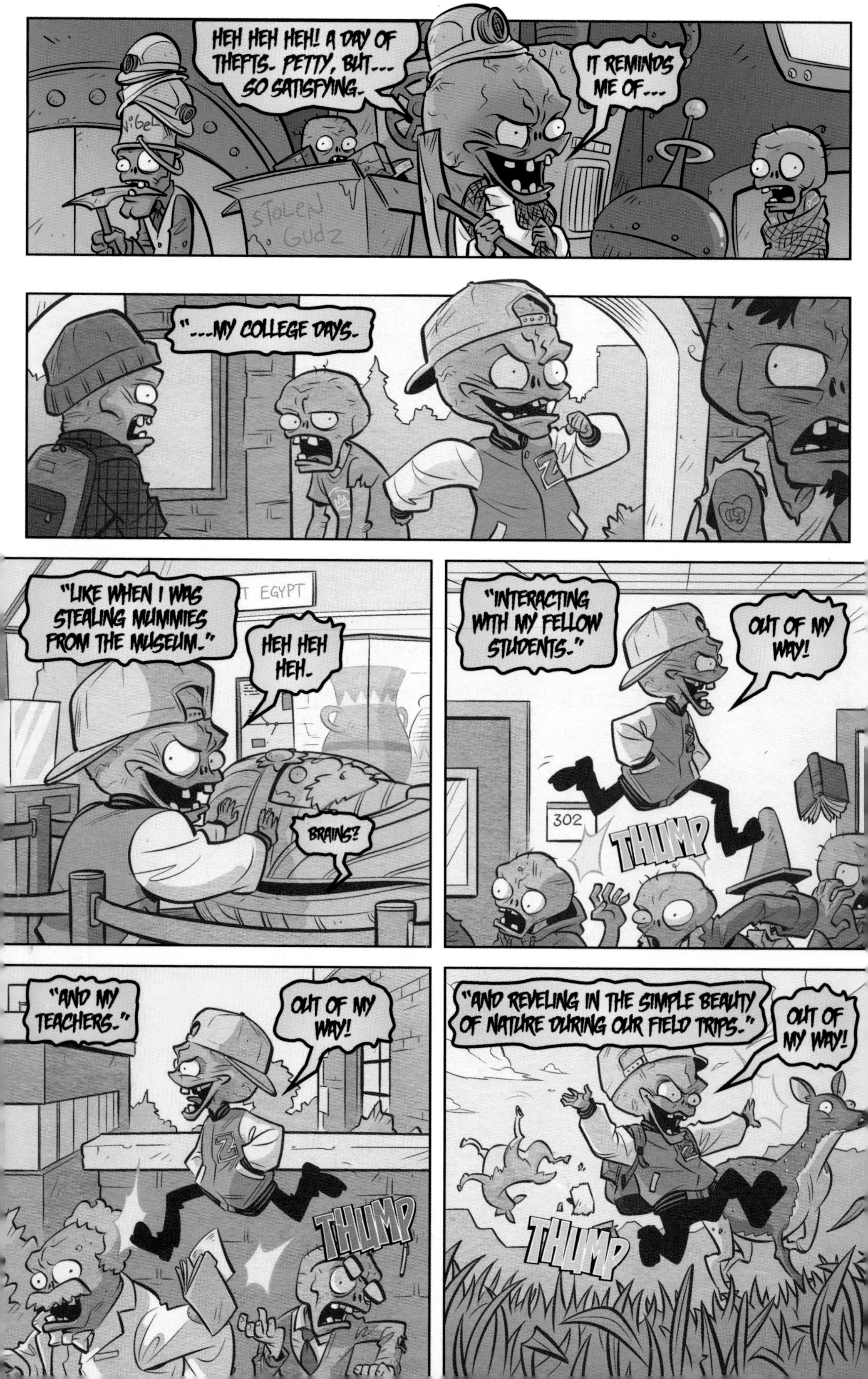
HEH HEH HEH! A DAY OF THEFTS. PETTY, BUT... SO SATISFYING.
IT REMINDS ME OF...
STOLEN GUDZ
"...MY COLLEGE DAYS."
"LIKE WHEN I WAS STEALING MUMMIES FROM THE MUSEUM."
T EGYPT
HEH HEH HEH.
BRAINS?
"INTERACTING WITH MY FELLOW STUDENTS."
OUT OF MY WAY!
302
THUMP
"AND MY TEACHERS."
OUT OF MY WAY!
THUMP
"AND REVELING IN THE SIMPLE BEAUTY OF NATURE DURING OUR FIELD TRIPS."
OUT OF MY WAY!
THUMP

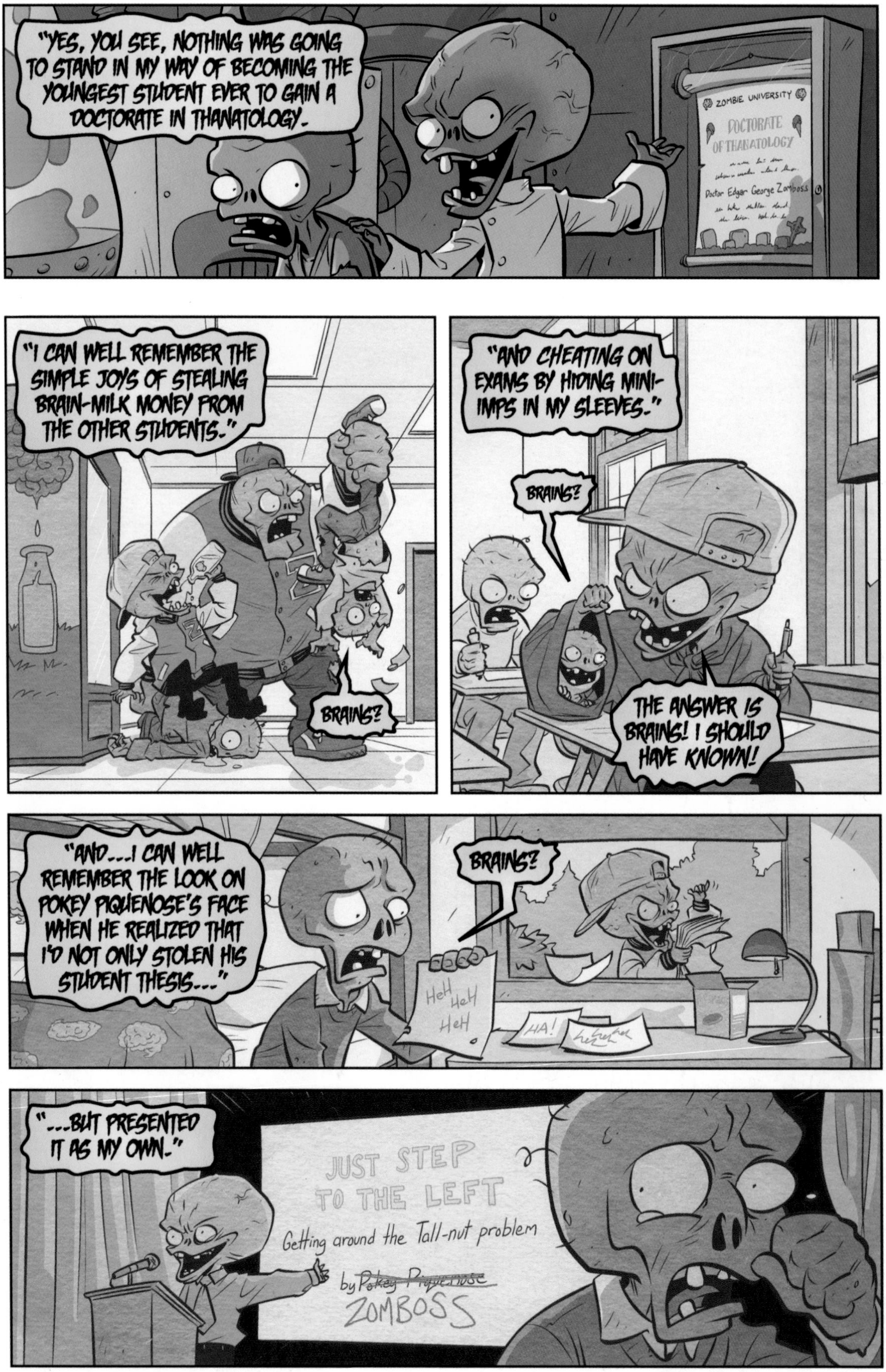
"YES, YOU SEE, NOTHING WAS GOING TO STAND IN MY WAY OF BECOMING THE YOUNGEST STUDENT EVER TO GAIN A DOCTORATE IN THANATOLOGY."
ZOMBIE UNIVERSITY
DOCTORATE OF THANATOLOGY
Doctor Edgar George Zomboss
"I CAN WELL REMEMBER THE SIMPLE JOYS OF STEALING BRAIN-MILK MONEY FROM THE OTHER STUDENTS."
BRAINS?
"AND CHEATING ON EXAMS BY HIDING MINI-IMPS IN MY SLEEVES."
BRAINS?
THE ANSWER IS BRAINS! I SHOULD HAVE KNOWN!
"AND... I CAN WELL REMEMBER THE LOOK ON POKEY PIQUENOSE'S FACE WHEN HE REALIZED THAT I'D NOT ONLY STOLEN HIS STUDENT THESIS..."
BRAINS?
HeH HeH HeH
HA!
"...BUT PRESENTED IT AS MY OWN."
JUST STEP TO THE LEFT
Getting around the Tall-nut problem
by ~~Pokey Piquenose~~
ZOMBOSS

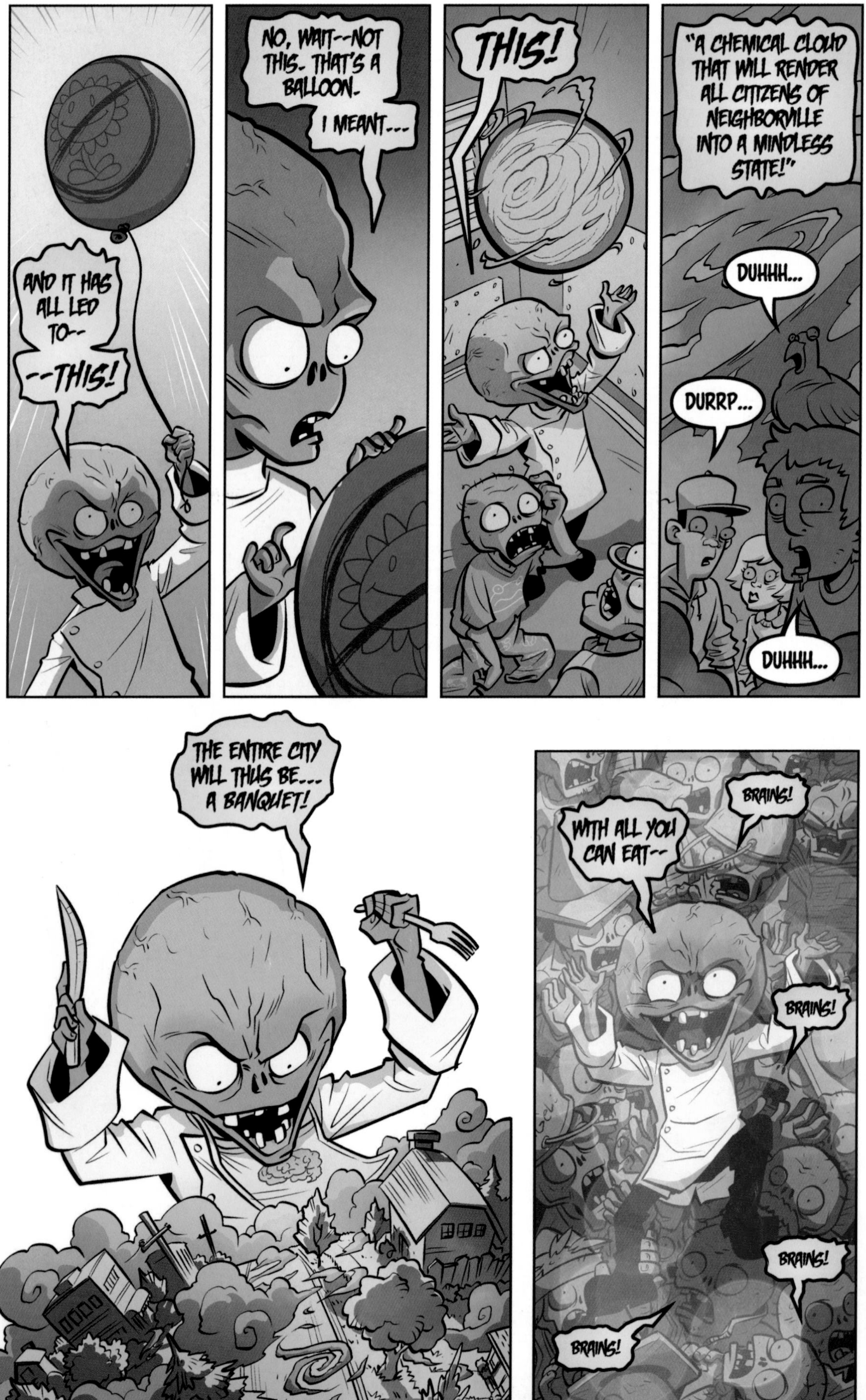
AND IT HAS ALL LED TO--
--THIS!
NO, WAIT--NOT THIS. THAT'S A BALLOON.
I MEANT...
THIS!
"A CHEMICAL CLOUD THAT WILL RENDER ALL CITIZENS OF NEIGHBORVILLE INTO A MINDLESS STATE!"
DUHHH...
DURRP...
DUHHH...
THE ENTIRE CITY WILL THUS BE... A BANQUET!
WITH ALL YOU CAN EAT--
BRAINS!
BRAINS!
BRAINS!
BRAINS!

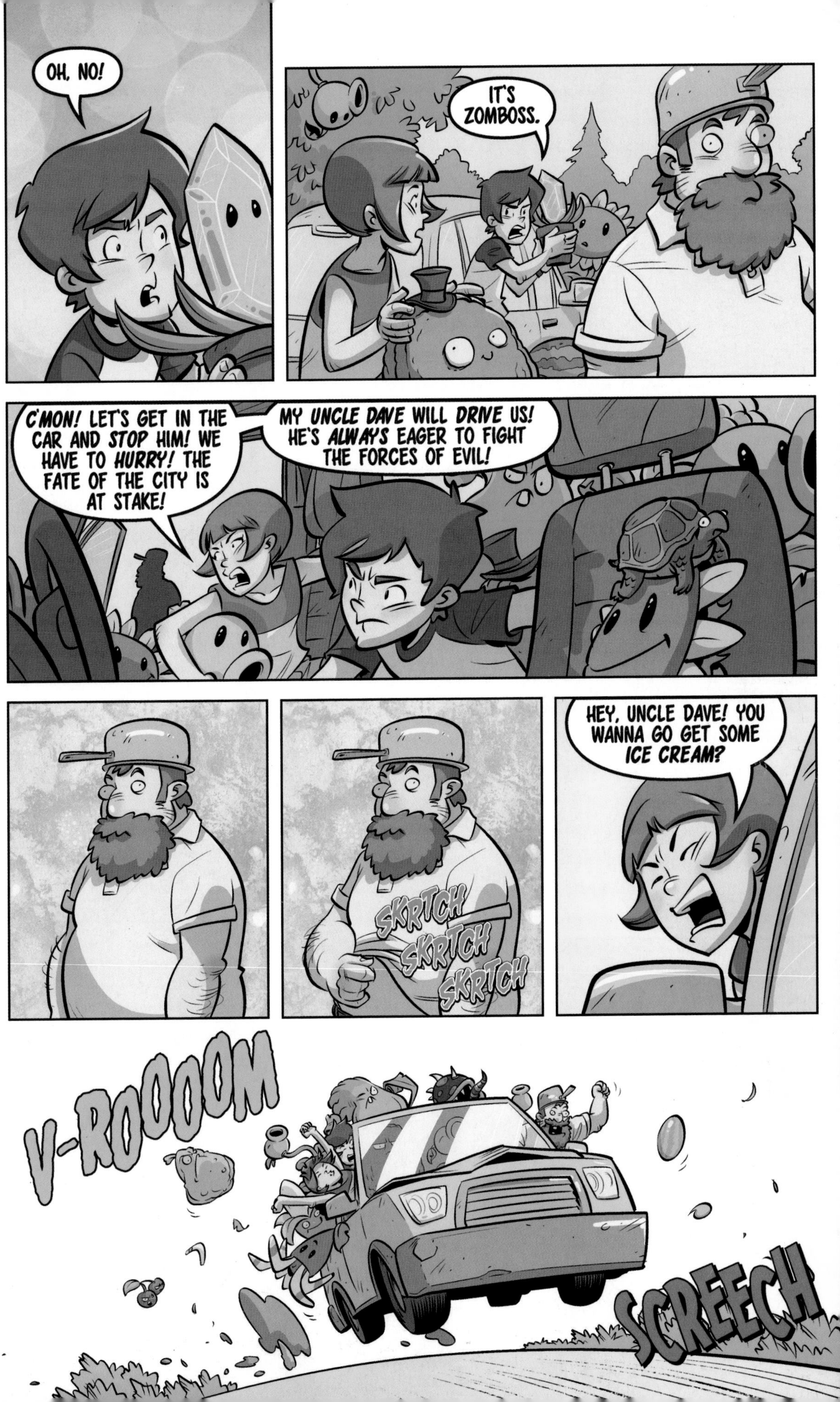
OH, NO!
IT'S ZOMBOSS.
C'MON! LET'S GET IN THE CAR AND STOP HIM! WE HAVE TO HURRY! THE FATE OF THE CITY IS AT STAKE!
MY UNCLE DAVE WILL DRIVE US! HE'S ALWAYS EAGER TO FIGHT THE FORCES OF EVIL!
SKRTCH
SKRTCH
SKRTCH
HEY, UNCLE DAVE! YOU WANNA GO GET SOME ICE CREAM?
V-ROOOOM
SCREECH

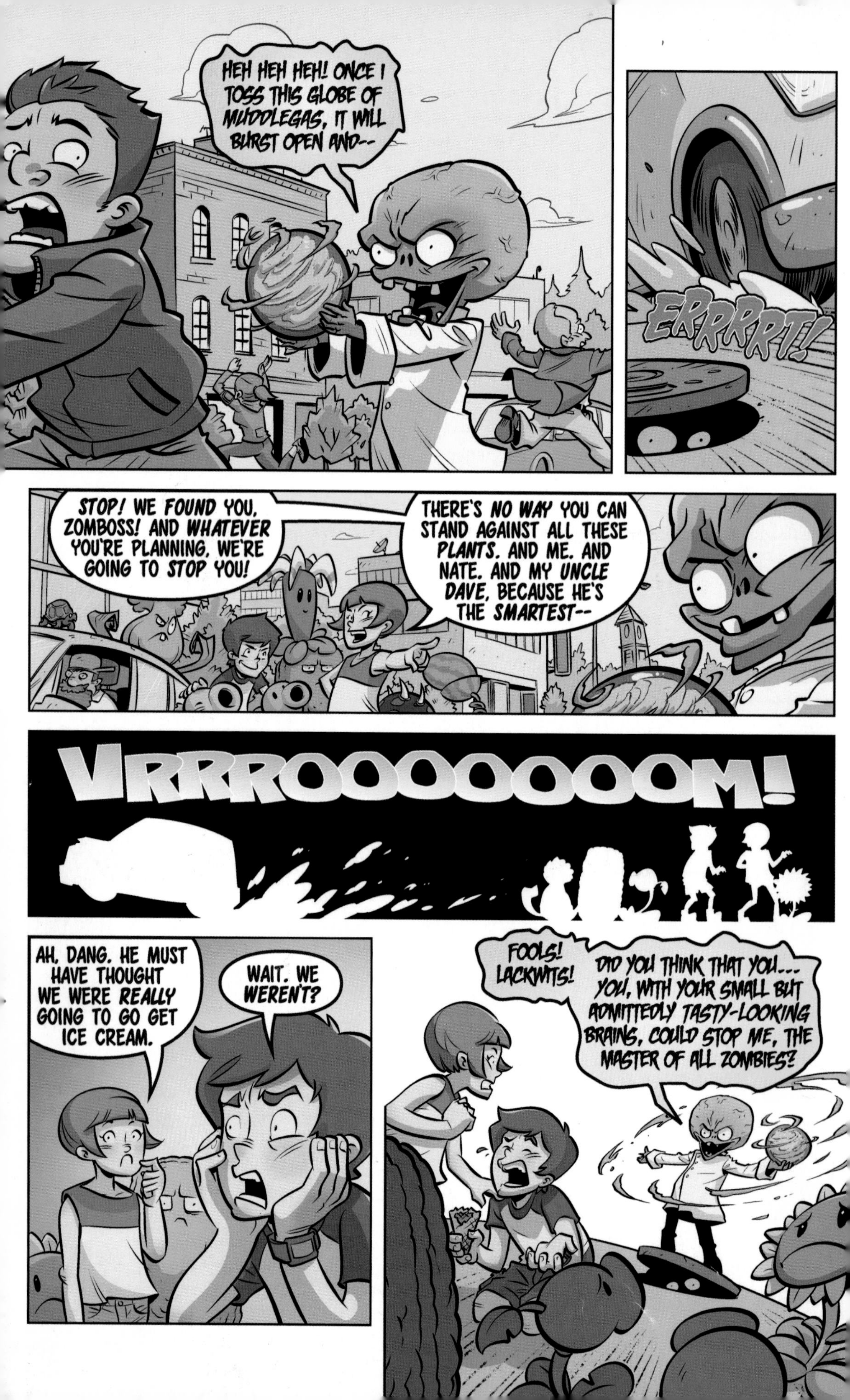
HEH HEH HEH! ONCE I TOSS THIS GLOBE OF MUDDLEGAS, IT WILL BURST OPEN AND--
ERRRRT!
STOP! WE FOUND YOU, ZOMBOSS! AND WHATEVER YOU'RE PLANNING, WE'RE GOING TO STOP YOU!
THERE'S NO WAY YOU CAN STAND AGAINST ALL THESE PLANTS. AND ME. AND NATE. AND MY UNCLE DAVE, BECAUSE HE'S THE SMARTEST--
VRRROOOOOOOOM!
AH, DANG. HE MUST HAVE THOUGHT WE WERE REALLY GOING TO GO GET ICE CREAM.
WAIT. WE WERENT?
FOOLS! LACKWITS!
DID YOU THINK THAT YOU... YOU, WITH YOUR SMALL BUT ADMITTEDLY TASTY-LOOKING BRAINS, COULD STOP ME, THE MASTER OF ALL ZOMBIES?

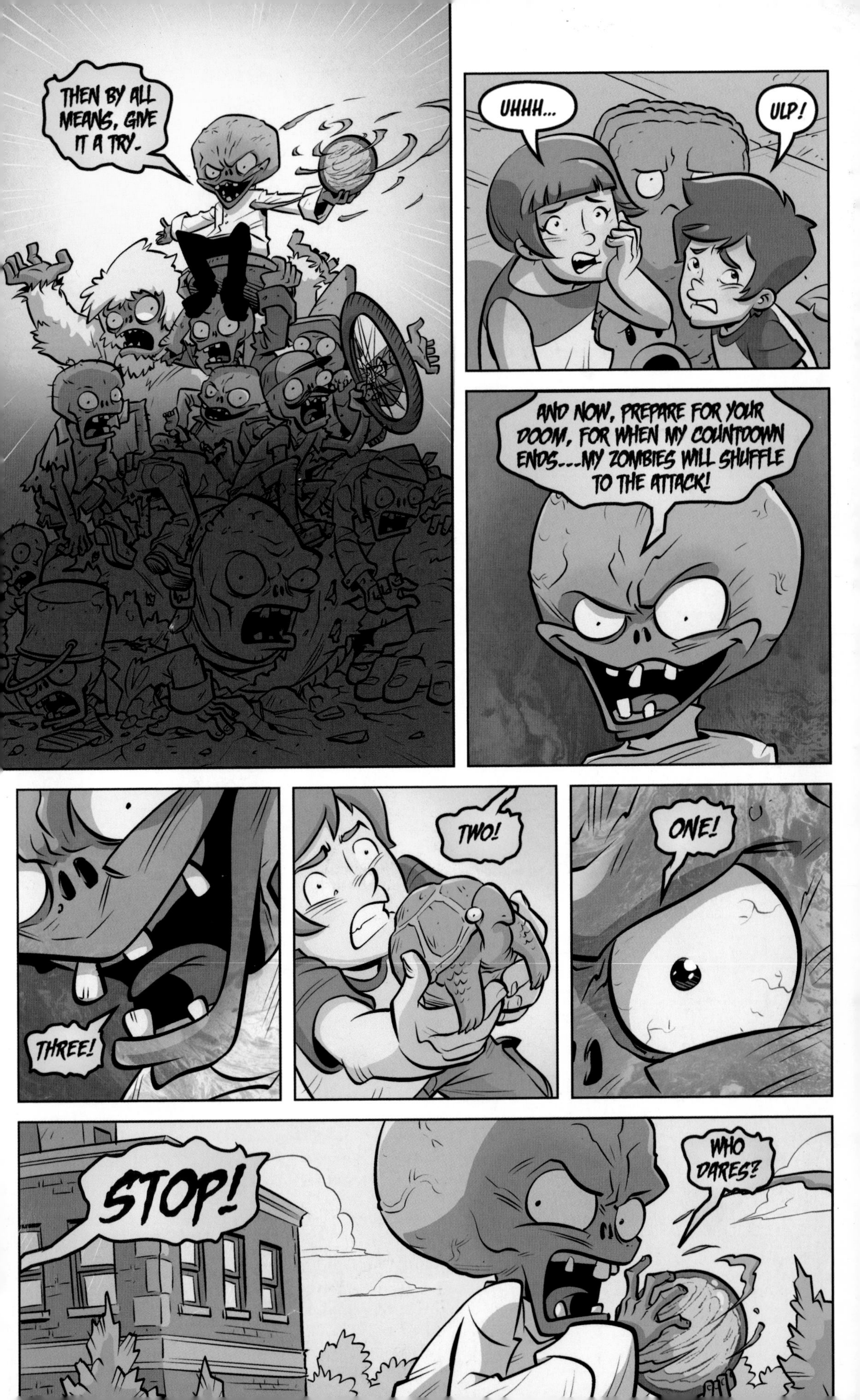
THEN BY ALL MEANS, GIVE IT A TRY.
UHHH...
ULP!
AND NOW, PREPARE FOR YOUR DOOM, FOR WHEN MY COUNTDOWN ENDS...MY ZOMBIES WILL SHUFFLE TO THE ATTACK!
THREE!
TWO!
ONE!
STOP!
WHO DARES?

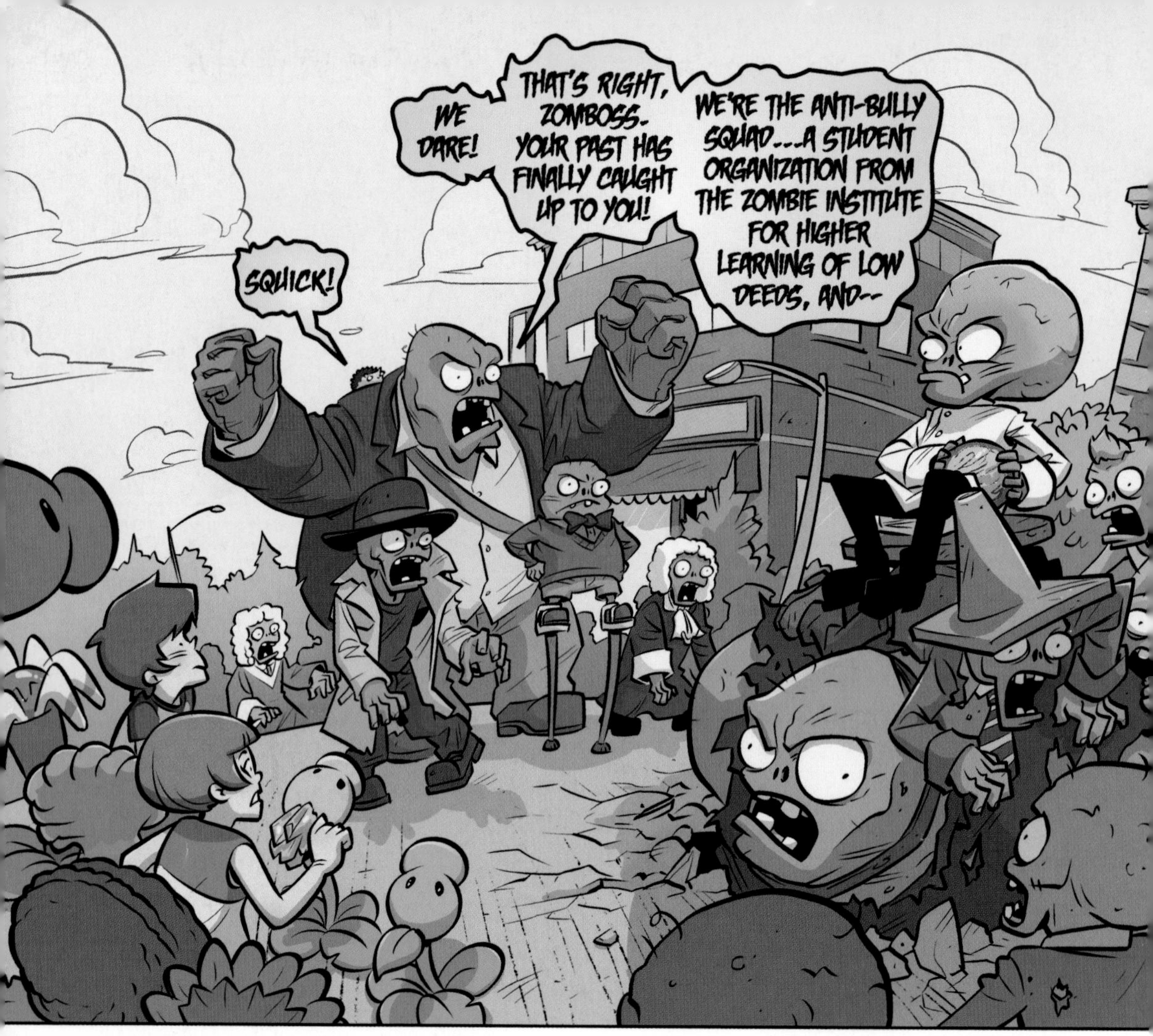
SQUICK!
WE DARE!
THAT'S RIGHT, ZOMBOSS. YOUR PAST HAS FINALLY CAUGHT UP TO YOU!
WE'RE THE ANTI-BULLY SQUAD...A STUDENT ORGANIZATION FROM THE ZOMBIE INSTITUTE FOR HIGHER LEARNING OF LOW DEEDS, AND--

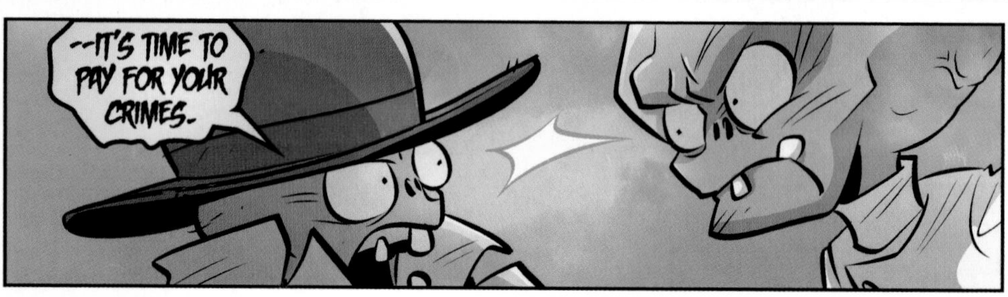
--IT'S TIME TO PAY FOR YOUR CRIMES.

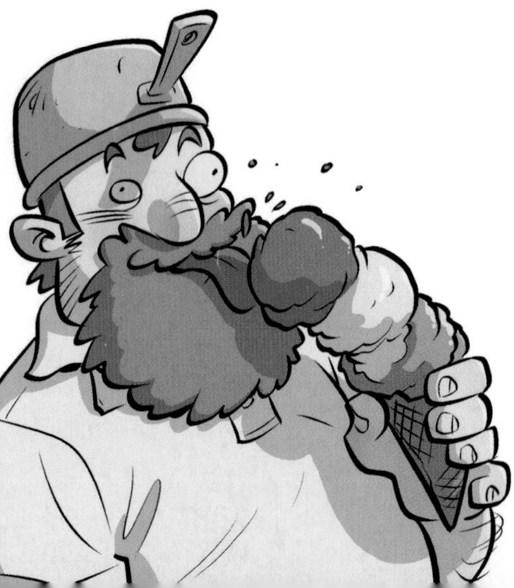

## CRAZY DAVE'S ICE-CREAM FACTS

DID YOU KNOW THAT ICE CREAM WAS INVENTED BY PENGUINS? IT'S TRUE! MAYBE. I DON'T KNOW. MAYBE ICE CREAM INVENTED PENGUINS? I LIKE THEM BOTH! HAVE YOU EVER SEEN AN ICE-CREAM-CONE-HEAD ZOMBIE? I HAVEN'T EITHER. STRAWBERRY ICE CREAM IS THE BEST FOR FUELING YOUR TIME MACHINE. *THESE ARE FACTS!*